No ....   Class ...... J

Author ... GRAVES S ....

Title .. Up in the tree ....

AN 3131234 9

First published in 2007 by
Franklin Watts
338 Euston Road
London
NW1 3BH

Franklin Watts Australia
Level 17/207 Kent Street
Sydney
NSW 2000

A CIP catalogue record for this book is available
from the British Library.

ISBN: 978 0 7496 7281 2 (hbk)
ISBN: 978 0 7496 7320 8 (pbk)

Series Editor: Jackie Hamley
Series Advisors: Dr Barrie Wade, Dr Hilary Minns
Series Designer: Peter Scoulding

Printed in China

Franklin Watts is a division of
Hachette Children's Books.

READING CORNER

PHONICS

Up in the Tree!

Illustrated by
Alexandra
Colombo

by
Sue Graves

W
FRANKLIN WATTS
LONDON • SYDNEY

Sue Graves
"Our cat used to run up trees and get stuck when she was a kitten. Luckily, she's more sensible now she's older!"

Alexandra Colombo
"My cat is called Pepi. He's a very big boy! I hope he doesn't get stuck up in a tree!"

The cat was up in the tree. Joe
saw her. "I will help you!" he said.

But he could not get
the cat down ...

7

... and then *he* could
not get down!

9

Dad saw Joe and the cat.

"I will help you!" he said.

11

But he could not get
them down ...

... and then *he* could not get down!

14

15

Mum saw Joe, Dad and the cat.

"I will help you!" she said.

But she could not get

them down ...

Suddenly, it began to rain and rain. It got very wet.

The cat ran down the tree.

She ran in the house.

Nobody came. They began
to shout louder.

His dad got them all down.

"We must get dry," said Mum.
Dad made tea.

They all had tea in the sun.

But the cat ...

... ran up the tree!

31

Notes for parents and teachers

READING CORNER PHONICS has been structured to provide maximum support for children learning to read through synthetic phonics. The stories are designed for independent reading but may also be used by adults for sharing with young children.

The teaching of early reading through synthetic phonics focuses on the 44 sounds in the English language, and how these sounds correspond to their written form in the 26 letters of the alphabet. Carefully controlled vocabulary makes these books accessible for children at different stages of phonics teaching, progressing from simple CVC (consonant-vowel-consonant) words such as "top" (t-o-p) to trisyllabic words such as "messenger" (mess-en-ger). READING CORNER PHONICS allows children to read words in context, and also provides visual clues and repetition to further support their reading. These books will help develop the all important confidence in the new reader, and encourage a love of reading that will last a lifetime!

If you are reading this book with a child, here are a few tips:

1. Talk about the story before you start reading. Look at the cover and the title. What might the story be about? Why might the child like it?

2. Encourage the child to reread the story, and to retell the story in their own words, using the illustrations to remind them what has happened.

3. Discuss the story and see if the child can relate it to their own experience, or perhaps compare it to another story they know.

4. Give praise! Small mistakes need not always be corrected. If a child is stuck on a word, ask them to try and sound it out and then blend it together again, or model this yourself. For example "wish" w-i-sh "wish".

READING CORNER PHONICS covers two grades of synthetic phonics teaching, with three levels at each grade. Each level has a certain number of words per story, indicated by the number of bars on the spine of the book:

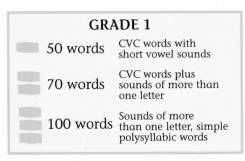

GRADE 1

	50 words	CVC words with short vowel sounds
	70 words	CVC words plus sounds of more than one letter
	100 words	Sounds of more than one letter, simple polysyllabic words

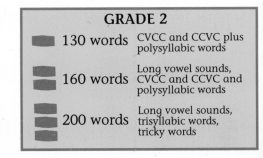

GRADE 2

	130 words	CVCC and CCVC plus polysyllabic words
	160 words	Long vowel sounds, CVCC and CCVC and polysyllabic words
	200 words	Long vowel sounds, trisyllabic words, tricky words